For Katherine.
With gratitude to Theodor Seuss Geisel
and my mom, Phyllis Fraser Cerf, who,
by teaming up to start Beginner Books,
taught us that learning to read
can be great fun.
—C.C.

Text copyright © 2019 by Christopher Cerf

Illustrations copyright © 2019 by Nicola Slater

All rights reserved. Published in the United States by Random House Children's Books,
a division of Penguin Random House LLC, New York.

Beginner Books, Random House, and the Random House colophon are registered trademarks
of Penguin Random House LLC. The Cat in the Hat logo ® and © Dr. Seuss Enterprises, L.P.
1957, renewed 1986. All rights reserved.

Visit us on the Web!
rhcbooks.com

Educators and librarians, for a variety of teaching tools, visit us at RHTeachersLibrarians.com

Library of Congress Cataloging-in-Publication Data
Names: Cerf, Christopher, author. | Slater, Nicola, illustrator.
Title: A skunk in my bunk! / by Christopher Cerf ; illustrated by Nicola Slater.
Description: First edition. | New York : Beginner Books, a division of Random House, [2019] |
Series: Beginner books | Summary: Illustrations and simple, cumulative text introduce such
characters as a pig in a wig dancing a jig, and a knight with a bright light saying good night.
Identifiers: LCCN 2018005498 | ISBN 978-0-525-57872-7 (trade) |
ISBN 978-0-525-57873-4 (lib. bdg.) | ISBN 978-0-525-57874-1 (ebook)
Subjects: | CYAC: Humorous stories.
Classification: LCC PZ7.C319 Sku 2019 | DDC [E]—dc23

Printed in the United States of America

10 9 8 7 6 5 4 3 2 1

First Edition

A SKUNK in My BUNK!

by Christopher Cerf

illustrated by Nicola Slater

BEGINNER BOOKS®
A Division of Random House

GOAT

GOAT
COAT

A goat in a coat.

GOAT
COAT
BOAT

A goat in a coat in a boat.

GOAT
COAT
BOAT
MOAT

A goat in a coat
in a boat in a moat.

BOAT
GOAT
COAT
MOAT
FLOAT

The boat with the goat
in the coat in the moat
does not float!

FISH
DISH

A fish on a dish.

TRISH
FISH
DISH
DELISH

Trish thinks the fish
on the dish
looks delish!

TRISH
WISH
FISH

Trish got her wish.
Now the fish
is in Trish!

PIG

PIG
WIG

A pig in a wig.

PIG
WIG
JIG

The pig
in the wig
is dancing
a jig!

TUB

CUB
TUB

"There's a cub
in my tub!"

CUB
TUB

"Go away, cub!
Get out of my tub!"

TUB
SCRUB

"Now I'M in my tub,
and it's MY turn to scrub!"

COP

COP
SHOP

A cop in a shop.

COP
SHOP
POP

A cop in a shop
with a bottle of pop.

COP
SHOP
POP
DROP

The cop in the shop

let the pop bottle drop!

COP
MOP
SOP
POP

The cop used a mop
to sop up the pop.

SLOP
POP
SHOP

Now the slop
from the pop
is gone
from my shop!

DUCK

DUCK
TRUCK

A duck in a truck.

DUCK
TRUCK
MUCK

The duck
drove the truck
into the muck.

DUCK
TRUCK
STUCK
MUCK

Now the duck
and the truck
are stuck
in the muck!

SMELL
YELL

"My bunk has a smell
that's so bad I could yell!"

SMELL
TELL

"Why does it smell?

I don't know. Can YOU tell?"

SKUNK
BUNK

"There's a skunk in my bunk!"

BUNK
STUNK

"THAT'S why my bunk stunk!"

KNIGHT

KNIGHT
NIGHT

A knight in the night.

KNIGHT
NIGHT
LIGHT
BRIGHT

The knight in the night
is holding a light . . .

. . . a light
that's so bright
that it lights
up the night.

The knight with the light
that is bright
waves good night.

And all those in sight
say "Good night!"
to the knight.